The Boy
Who Sat By
The Window

HELPING CHILDREN
COPE WITH
VIOLENCE

Written by
Chris Loftis
Illustrations by
Catharine Gallagher

1

2

Library of Congress Catalog Card Number: 96-68929

Loftis, Chris.
   The Boy Who Sat By The Window

ISBN: 0-88282-147-4
SMALL HORIZONS
A Division of New Horizon Press

2001 2000 1999 1998 1997 / 54321

Printed in Hong Kong

3

Author's note

I believe that children make decisions every day that affect their lives forever. They decide whom to follow, who they want to be like, and with what they want to be involved by gauging the success they see in others. We, as adults may not know it, but children watch everything we do. They listen to what we say. They decide if we have a message worth hearing. They decide if we are worth following.

In my work with Big Brothers/Big Sisters, I have seen countless children benefit from the loving care and guidance of an adult friend and role model. Of all the organizations with which I have had the privilege of working, Big Brothers/Big Sisters is a shining example of a program that works. It makes a difference, one child at a time.

Still, one day, a few years ago, we received news that nearly broke the hearts of agency personnel and the people of the community. A boy, one of our "Little Brothers" had been killed while walking home from school. It was not an accident. A carload of young people, most of them children, had stopped and killed him just a block from his home. His offense: he was wearing the wrong color shirt, on the wrong day, when the wrong group of kids drove by....

The family was devastated, as were the boy's schoolmates, and the entire community. In our small town, the world had, suddenly and for all, become a much more dangerous place.

In my sorrow for his loss and in my anger at the people responsible, I thought of how different and how much better our little world would have been if just one of the teenagers in that car had **heard** someone tell them, "there's just no reason for this to happen." If someone who had power and resonance in their lives could have offered them guidance and friendship, perhaps the only thing that would have happened is that on a sunny day, in a little town in Washington State, a boy in a red shirt would have enjoyed an uneventful walk home from school.

Spurred by that tragedy, I wrote this story. It is based, not on that little boy's murder, but on the lives of the people he left behind. Sadly, as this situation is replayed all across our country, there are families and friends of little boys being left behind in almost every city and town.

That must end.

You see, I believe that nothing justifies violence against a child. It bares repeating, if only one of the young attackers, now appropriately serving long terms in prison, had had a parent, relative, neighbor, "Big Brother" or "Big Sister"...anyone who would have convinced him that violence is not the answer to problems or a means to attaining his desires, our community would not have endured such pain and despair.

Most importantly, our community would not have lost the little boy who sat by the window....

There was music in the hallway.
Someone
was playing his stereo.
Joshua thought it very strange,
that on a day like today
with such bad news in the air,
there would still be such a range....

7

...of emotions and activities.
Some people
acted like nothing had happened at all.
They went about their normal day
and even played music in the hall.

8

Others
sat at their desks crying.
Joshua thought he'd seen the teacher crying too.
You see,
this morning,
the little boy who sits by the window
was shot and killed while riding his bike to school.

When Joshua first got to school,
he saw police cars and an ambulance
and a big fire truck with a ladder on top.
There were newspaper reporters talking to all the children
and there were television cameras set up.

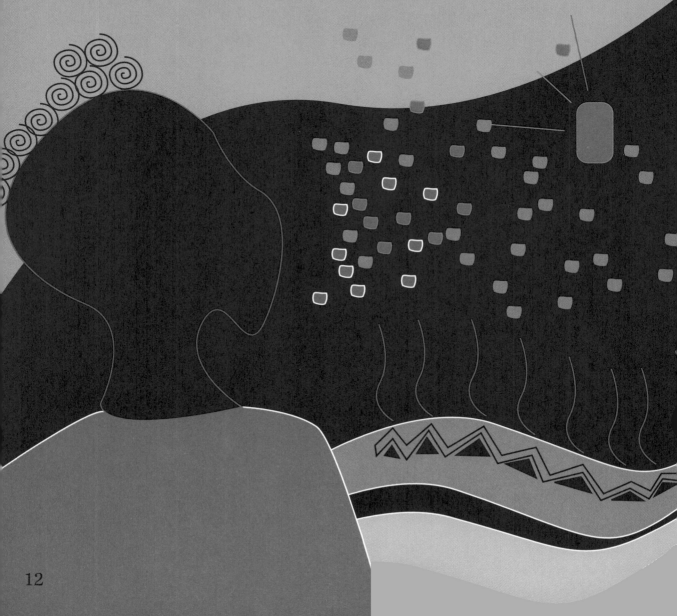

There were teachers everywhere,
telling the students to stay calm
and to go inside their rooms.
In the middle of all of this commotion,
a group of people
stood in a circle looking down,
their faces filled with sorrow,
their faces filled with gloom.

Then a car pulled up with two women inside,
one,
still in her pajamas and house coat.
A policeman
ran over to the older of the two.
He reached out, grabbed her arm,
and then he hurriedly spoke.

14

That's when
the woman
just started screaming.
She kept calling out the little boy's name.
She ran
to where the crowd was standing.
She looked down.
Joshua knew
her life
would
never
be the same.

16

You see,
the little boy who sat by the window
was more than just a little boy.
He was more than a child who had a red bicycle.
He was more than someone who shared his toys.

He was more than a child in a lunch line.
He was more than an infielder on a team.
He was the lady's son.
He was her family.
The little boy was her hopes
  and her dreams.

17

Joshua remembered
the boy by the window.
He remembered him as sort of shy
but always polite.
Really,
until this sad day,
he was just a face in the crowd...
his voice, just a sound...
his face, just a sight.

Now,
everyone was talking about him,
what he did and didn't do.
Who were his friends?
What did he like?
Who knew him outside of school?

19

There were rumors everywhere.
Everyone
had an idea of who might have done this and why.
Some talked loudly
of what they'd do if they caught the person responsible.
Some
just put their heads down on their desks.
Some
just cried.

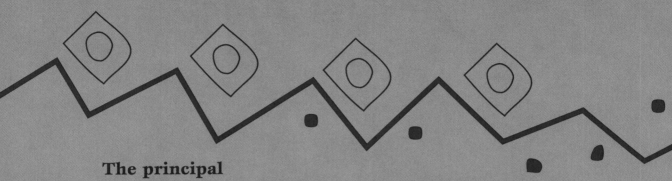

The principal
allowed everyone to call home
and suggested to the teachers
that there not be much work done that day.
The school district sent over some counselors
and anyone who wished to talk to them could stay.

By lunch time,
half of the children had gone home.
Their parents came and took them away.
This sort of thing had never happened
around here before.
So,
no one knew
what he or she should say.

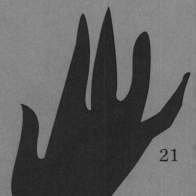

There were ministers, priests, and rabbis.
The school seemed a river of sad expressions,
and in every glance
there was a look of confusion,
like a teacher
who has lost the point of a lesson.

There were looks of sorrow,
        looks of confusion,
            looks of anger,
                looks of fear,
looks of worry and trepidation.
    That's how you feel
        when you're lost
            and the way is not clear...

There were just so many people
with so much to say
that Joshua
became nervous
and very afraid...

...and when his mother and father
knocked on the door of his class,
he looked up to them
and then ran.
He ran very hard.
He ran very fast.

For the first time,
he began crying.
He cried so hard that it hurt his face.
He wanted to go home.
He wanted to leave.
He wanted to leave this sad and terrible place.

His mother was crying as well.
His father was trying not to let it show.
They hurriedly went to the car,
got in
and then
headed down the road.

When they got home,
they all
just sat there outside.
They all
held one another tight.
Then they went in,
and built a fire in the fireplace.
You could actually hear
the sound
of the quiet.

No one knew what to say
and so thankfully,
no one even tried.
Joshua
thought about the little boy's mother.
Joshua
thought about the little boy.
Joshua thought.
Joshua cried.

The details came out slowly.
For a while there was nothing new.
Then, a few days later,
there was a story in the newspaper.
It said there had been some sort of breakthrough.

The police had arrested four people,
all of them
members of the same gang.
The oldest was seventeen
and all of them
had recognizable names.

Joshua
actually knew two of the boys.
One lived right down the street.
They all went to a nearby high school.
There had been times
When he might have seen them at the store
or would have said hello
when they chanced to meet.

They were all
just neighborhood kids,
at least until that dreadful day...
when as part of some kind of gang thing
they went out,
but that time
they didn't go out to play.

No, they went out to hurt someone.
They boasted
they were going to hurt someone bad...
and the first someone to whom they came
was a little boy on a red bicycle.
They yelled at him
and scared the little lad.

Then,
someone
fired a gun.
The newspaper article didn't say who.
The boys say now that they were just playing,
just trying to scare the boy...
the boy
who sat by the window
at Joshua's school.

Several months went by.
Somehow,
things got back to normal,
at least in the homes of people not directly involved.
The police put the story together.
The article in the newspaper
said the case was now solved.

The teacher
assigned someone else
to the chair by the window.
She said,
"We all have to get on with our lives."
The school was back to normal,
as busy
as a big, busy bee hive.

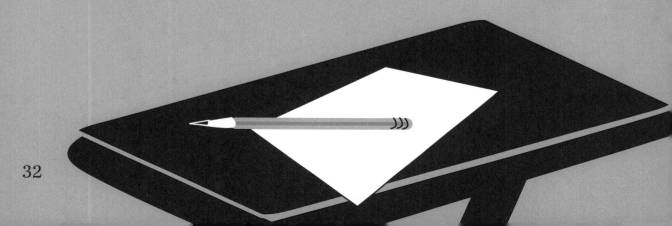

Joshua's parents
dropped him off more often, though.
They didn't want him
to walk alone to school.
Dad even changed his work schedule,
so he could pick Joshua up on Mondays and Wednesdays.
Mom was going to pick him up on Tuesday, too.

Slowly,
Joshua began to forget about that day,
the boy on the bicycle,
          the boys in the car.
As Mom said,
"You can't live in the past if you want to live at all.
You've got to learn to live right where you are..."

A few months later,
Joshua and his mother
stopped at the grocery store
on their way home.
Then Joshua turned down Aisle Three
and bumped into a lady.
He looked up
and saw it was Mrs. Jones.

She was the mother
of one of the boys in the car,
the one that lived on Joshua's street.
She smiled at him and gave Joshua a hug.
She said,
"I'm glad we've had a chance to meet."

Joshua pulled away a little bit.
He was really kind of afraid.
He hadn't seen Mrs. Jones
since before the shooting
and Joshua
had no earthly idea what he should say.

Joshua was nervous.
Mrs. Jones looked at him standing there.
Then, she reached down,
patted his head,
and
playfully messed up his hair.

She said,
"Joshua,
 how are you doing?"
Joshua said nothing.
Mrs. Jones just smiled.
Then, she knelt down and said softly,
"It's alright, hon;
I'm afraid
no one's going to know
what to say to me for a while."

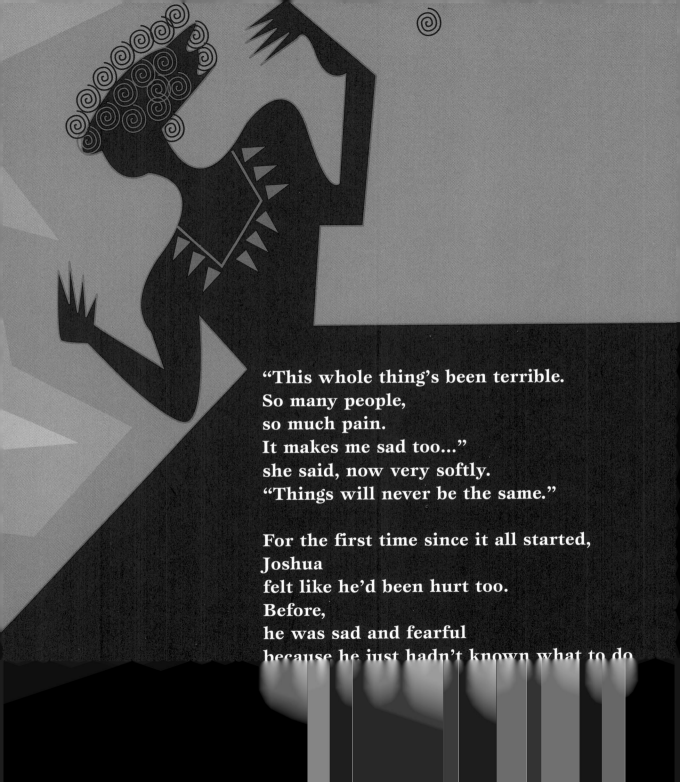

"This whole thing's been terrible.
So many people,
so much pain.
It makes me sad too..."
she said, now very softly.
"Things will never be the same."

For the first time since it all started,
Joshua
felt like he'd been hurt too.
Before,
he was sad and fearful
because he just hadn't known what to do

40

Now,
Joshua realized something...
EVERYBODY
had been harmed that day...
not just the boy who sat by the window,
or his mom,
or the kids who had all been so afraid.

The parents of the boys who did the shooting,
the parents of the children now afraid,
the schools officials that now
had to deal with the violence,
where once, they worried only about
where children played...

The police,
who had to arrest children,
the judge,
who had to put them in jail,
the mothers of those boys now in prison...
with dreams for their children's future
now doomed to fail.

Everybody...
everybody was hurt,
and Joshua once again felt the need to cry.
Mrs. Jones picked him up
and sat down at a table.
She said,
"We've got to stop this pain, Josh.
We've got to do better
than just try.

"Now listen here, child
and listen good.
I'm going to tell you something
about childhood.

"It should be filled with joy.
It should be filled with smiles.
But here
what should be and what is
separated
by miles
and miles.

"There's just no reason
in this whole,
wide world
why ANYBODY
should harm a little boy
or a little girl.

42

43

"And surely
it isn't right for children
to kill children
over
  things
    that
      don't
        really
          matter...
like the color of someone's clothes
or the color of someone's skin
or where you stand on some stupid
social ladder.

44

"This kind of violence
has got to stop
and I'll tell you something else that's true.
It's got to end right now
and its ending starts right here,
with me
and with you.

"YOU
decide now YOU're not going to harm anyone.
YOU decide now it's wrong.
YOU decide now
to make your life a good one.
YOU decide now you're going to live long.

"Violence has no place in a child's life.
In your family or mine.
It's a kind of treason.
Children,
STOP believing
that you get more by taking,
because
there is just
no
reason."

Mrs. Jones grew silent.
Joshua
looked up into her eyes.
In them, he saw
the faraway look
grown people sometimes get
when their dreams
and their tears
collide.

Joshua went home.
First he hugged his mom.
Then he hugged his dad.
He walked around the house and
looked at all they had...

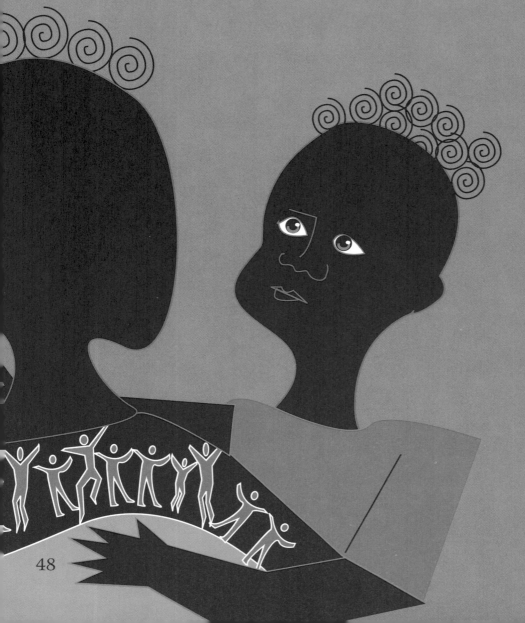

Oh, more than the stuff
that filled the rooms,
more than the car
out in the drive...
Joshua
realized the greatest things he had
was that his family loved him
and the fact that he was alive.

That meant he had tomorrows
to do the things he wanted to do,
and if those dreams fell by the wayside,
he could find other dreams
and make them come true.

Whatever was going to happen,
he wanted to be there.
He wanted to take part....
Whatever was going to happen
he wanted to be with those he loved.
He wanted to always share their hearts.

Finally,
Joshua thought of Mrs. Jones
and what she would face in the coming seasons....
How she was right
when she said,
"We have to
  stop
    this
      violence.
Because, very simply, children...
                    there's just no reason."

*Thank you
for sharing
this story with me.*

Chris Loftis